The
Spider
Who
Created
the
World

by Amy MacDonald
pictures by G. Brian Karas

Orchard Books   New York

When the sky was
young and the world
just a dream, when
the stars were still
learning their names,
a spider named Nobb
came floating through
the Air, at the end
of a long, soft thread.

On her back was
a white, white egg.

"I need someplace
to set my egg," said
Nobb, looking all
about. "The time is
near for it to hatch."

"You may set your
egg on me," sighed
the Air.

"You are kind," said
Nobb, "but I need
somewhere firm,
somewhere out of
the wet and the cold."

So she called to the Moon:

"O Moon, floating free, I need somewhere to live. May I stop for a while on your brow?"

But the Moon frowned and said, "Go away from here, Nobb, with your tiny sharp fangs. There's no room for you in my home."

Nobb was as patient
as a hundred spiders,
so she called to the
Sun:

"O Sun, floating free,
I need somewhere to
live. May I stop for a
while by your
hearth?"

But the Sun
shuddered and said,
"Go away from here,
Nobb, with your
sticky white thread.
There's no room for
you in my home."

Now Nobb felt as sad
as a hundred spiders,
but she called to the
Cloud:

"O Cloud, floating free,
I need somewhere to
live. May I stop for a
while on your lap?"

But the Cloud gasped
and said, "Go away
from here, Nobb,
with your eight itchy
legs. There's no room
for you in my home."

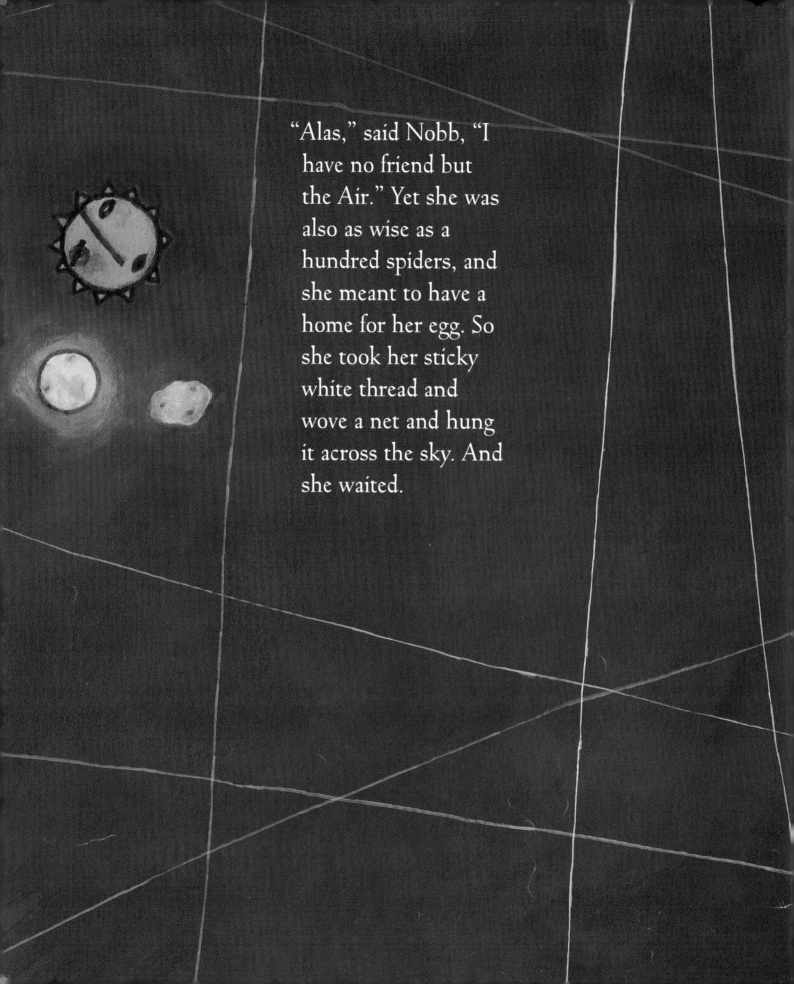

"Alas," said Nobb, "I
have no friend but
the Air." Yet she was
also as wise as a
hundred spiders, and
she meant to have a
home for her egg. So
she took her sticky
white thread and
wove a net and hung
it across the sky. And
she waited.

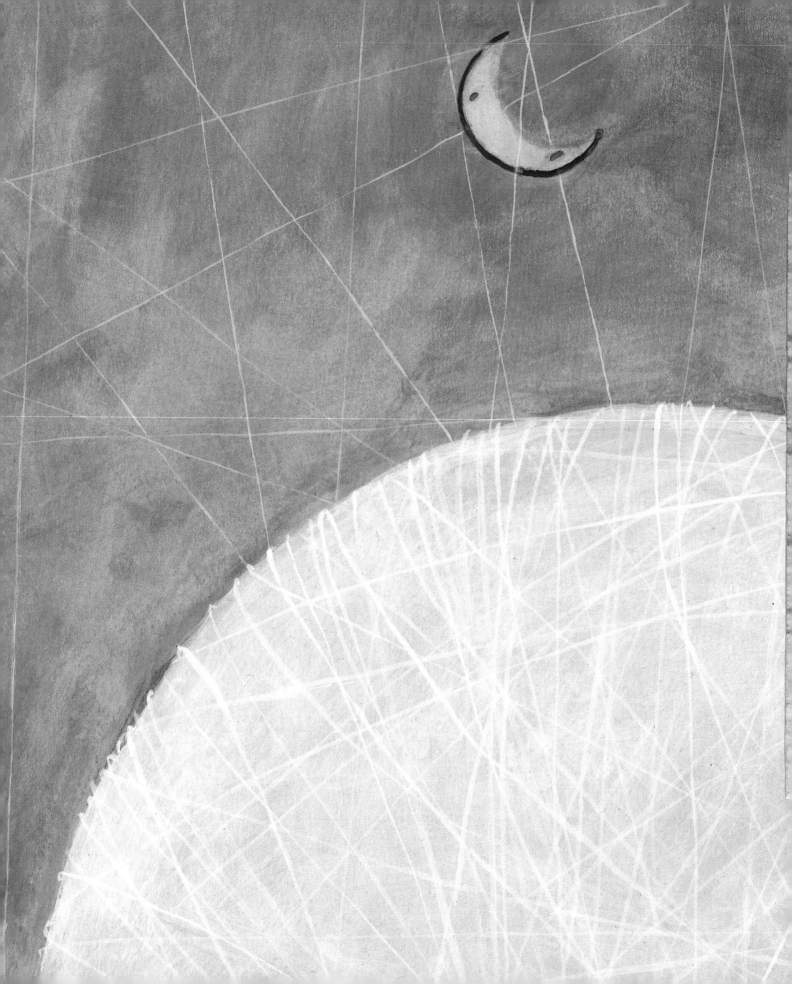

First the Moon came
along on its path
through the sky and
got caught tight in
Nobb's web.

"Set me free!" begged
the Moon.

"All in good time," said
Nobb. And with her
tiny sharp fangs she
sliced off a piece from
the side of the Moon
and wrapped it up
neatly with her thread.

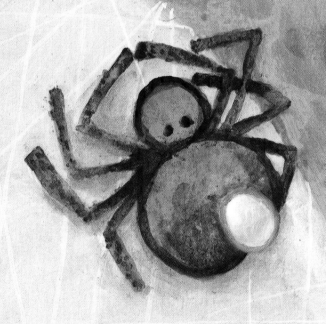

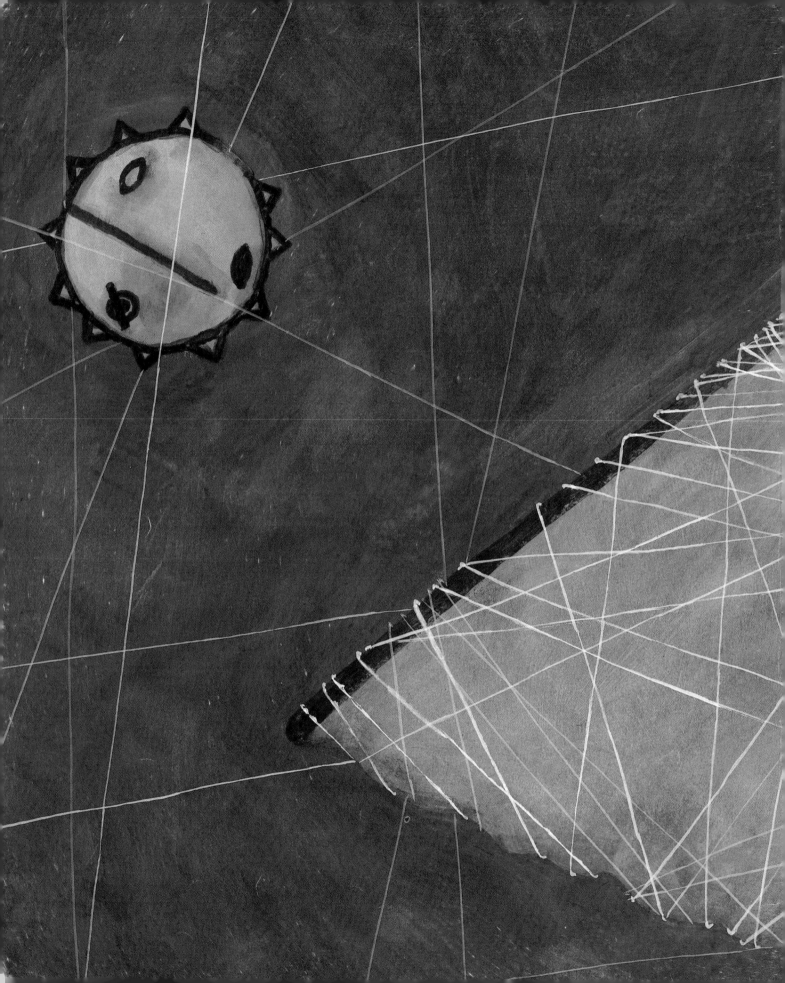

Next the Sun came along and was quickly caught in Nobb's web.

"Set me free!" begged the Sun.

"All in good time," said Nobb. But first she sliced off a piece of the Sun and wrapped it up neatly with her sticky white thread.

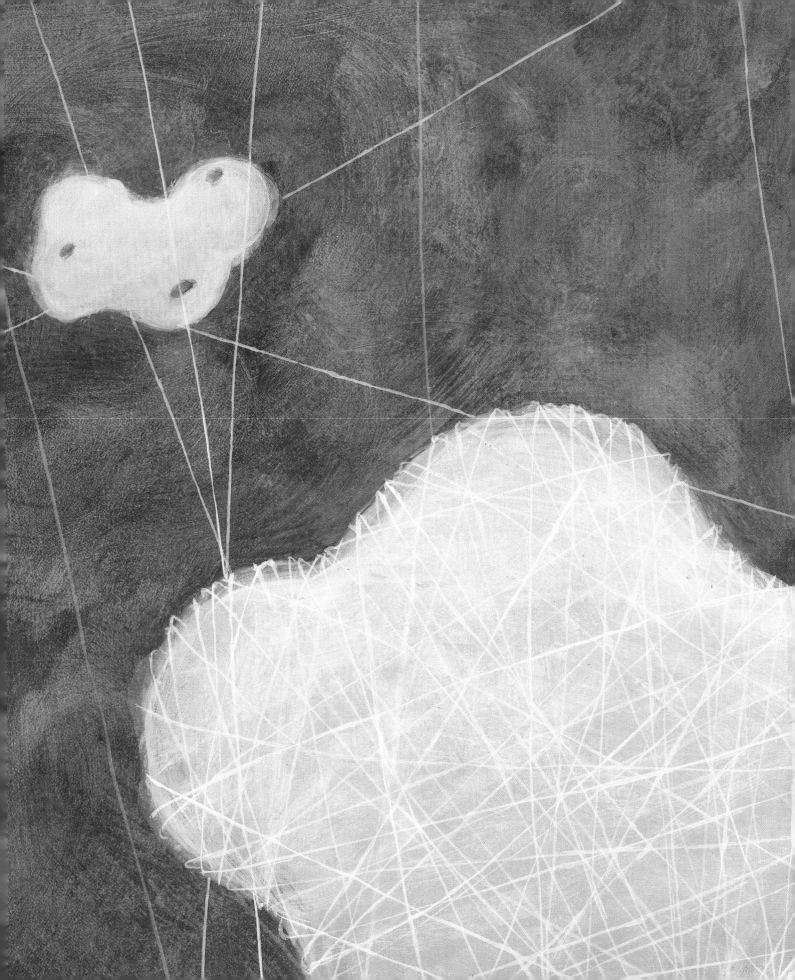

Last to come was the
Cloud, and soon it,
too, was caught in the
web.

"Set me free!" begged
the Cloud.

"All in good time,"
said Nobb. But first
she sliced off a piece
of the Cloud and
wrapped it up neatly
with her eight itchy
legs.

Now Nobb was as
clever as a hundred
spiders. With her
fangs and her thread
she took the piece of
Moon and wrapped it
round and round the
piece of Sun. In this
way she made the
Earth with the Fire
inside it.

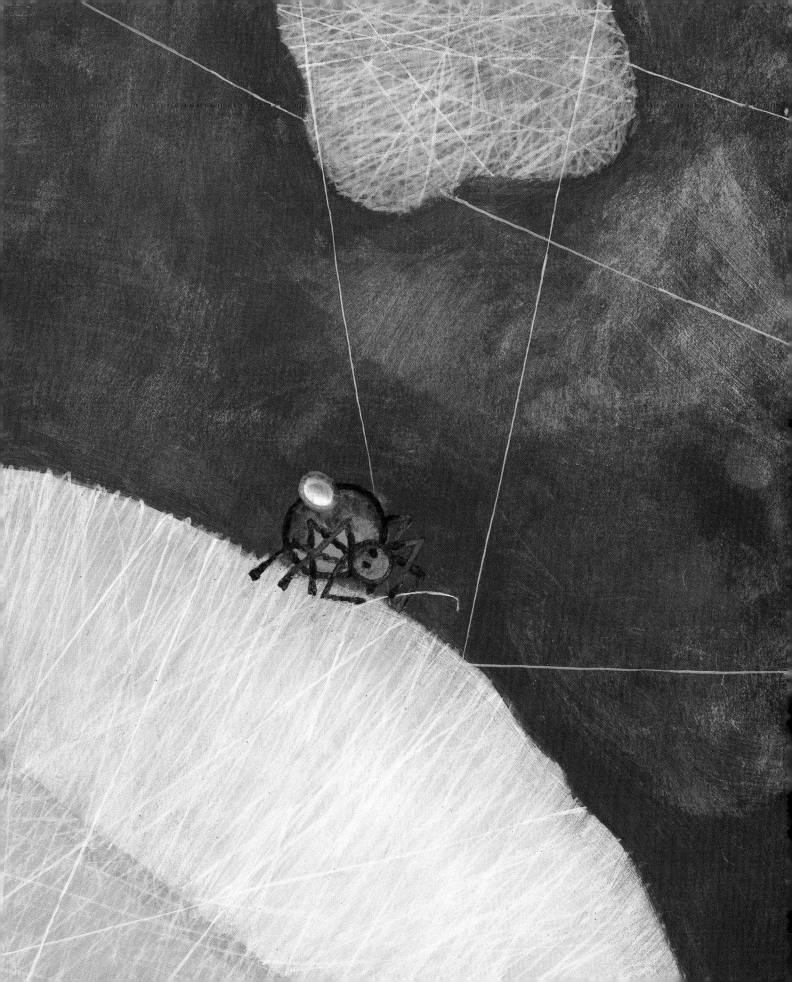

Next she took the bit
of Cloud and
squeezed it between
her eight itchy legs
until all the juice ran
out. In this way she
made the Water and
oceans that cover the
Earth.

"At last I have a home
for my egg," she said.

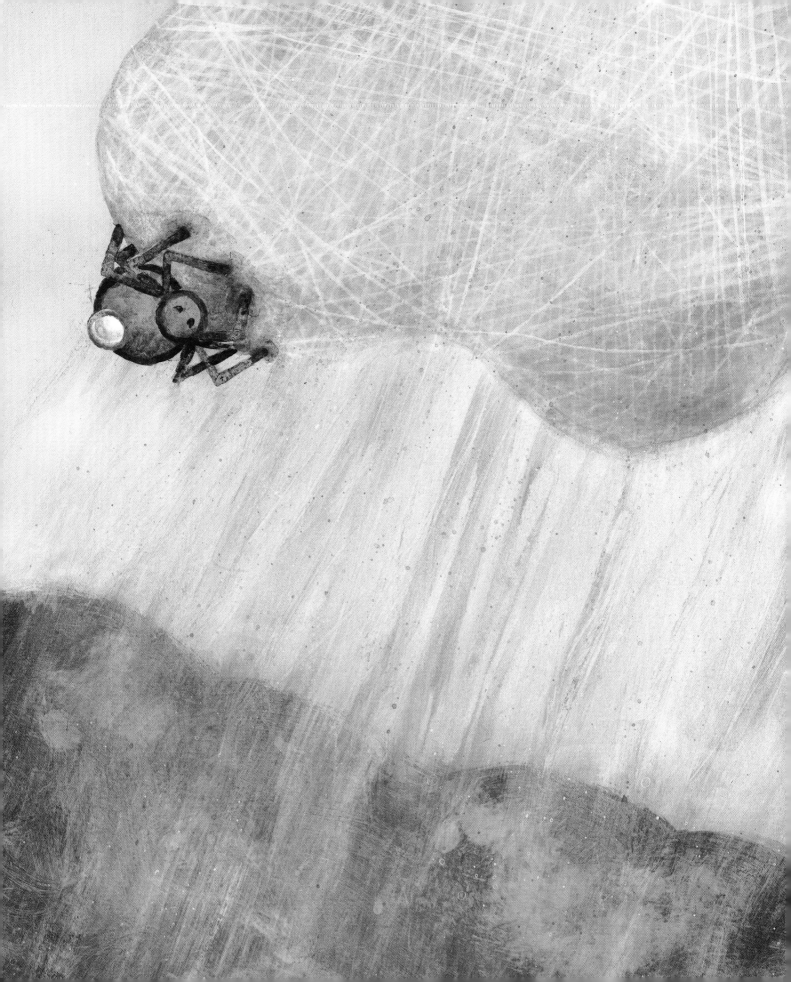

Then she laid her white, white egg
between two great mountains.

And from this egg hatched out not just spiderlings but birds of the Air and fishes of the Water and beasts of the land and all the beings — small and big — that fill the world to this day.

And to this day the
Moon and Sun and
Cloud still float above
the Earth — though
every now and then,
if you look very
closely, you just
might see where
Nobb took a bite.

As for Nobb, though she made the Earth, the Fire, and the Water, she never forgot who was her only friend. And that is why she lives, still and always, up in the Air, suspended halfway between the land and the sea and the stars.

For Susan Hand Shetterly —A.M.

For Zachary —G.B.K.

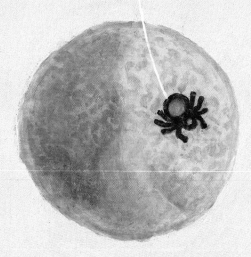

Text copyright © 1996 by Amy MacDonald

Illustrations copyright © 1996 by G. Brian Karas

Orchard Books
95 Madison Avenue
New York, NY 10916

Manufactured in the United States of America
Printed by Barton Press, Inc.   Bound by Horowitz/Rae
Book design by Chris Hammill Paul

10 9 8 7 6 5 4 3 2 1

The text of this book is set in 20 point Truesdell.   The illustrations are acrylic and gouache paintings.

Library of Congress Cataloging-in-Publication Data

MacDonald, Amy.
    The spider who created the world / by Amy MacDonald ; pictures by G. Brian Karas.
        p. cm.
    "A Melanie Kroupa book."
    Summary: Spider needs a firm place to set her egg which is about to hatch, but since sun, moon, and cloud tell
her they have no room for it, she creates the world.
    ISBN 0-531-09505-3. — ISBN 0-531-08855-3 (lib. bdg.)
    [1. Spiders—Fiction. 2. Creation—Fiction.] I. Karas, G. Brian, ill. II. Title.
PZ7.M1463Sp 1996
    [E]—dc20   95-23181